WRITTEN BY RACHEL ROSE GRAY AND TRICIA O'NEILL POLITTE

ILLUSTRATED BY KIM SPONAUGLE

Halo
PUBLISHING
INTERNATIONAL

For all our readers:

Thank you for following Joy. It might take time, but Joy and her friends are confident that you can also defeat any darkness that shadows your life. Let your light shine!

ISBN: 978-1-63765-004-2
LCCN: 2021906466

Halo Publishing International

Halo Publishing International, LLC
8000 W Interstate 10, Suite 600
San Antonio, Texas 78230
www.halopublishing.com

Printed and bound in the United States of America

THIS BOOK IS ESPECIALLY FOR:

Chapter 1

"Joy, your mother and I are so proud of you," Papa says as he pats my leg. "Every day for weeks you've been making farmers happy by singing in their fields to make their crops grow."

We are in the royal coach, bumping along as we return to the palace. The queen insists that Mama, Papa, and I use her coach when we travel to farms. I have to admit it is pretty grand, and it beats walking.

I nod my head, as we pass an apple orchard now with thousands of tiny white blossoms on the trees. They *are* nicer to look at than bare, brown branches.

"Your singing brought the sunshine back into the kingdom. That's a very big deal." Papa beams with pride.

"Not at the palace," I mumble. "There never seems to be sunshine at the palace."

"Well . . .," Papa begins, but I sit up and finally tell them what's been bugging me.

"It's always dark at the palace, inside and out. It's like a big, dark cloud, like a dragon, hangs over it. The queen ordered us here, but she never really talks to us. I miss my friends. I want to go back home and see Mia and Henry!" I am trying not to cry.

Mama quickly shifts from her seat and pulls me into a hug. I can feel her warm breath on my bald head.

Yep, I'm bald. Not a hair on my head. No one really knows why. I used to wear a scarf to hide it, but now nobody seems to care, so I don't wear it anymore.

"I know it's been tough for you. Sometimes we have to give up what we want for a short time, so others can be happy for a long time. Hopefully, we will be finished here soon, and the queen will let us return home," Mama says in her soothing voice.

"It *is* tough, and I'm just a kid!" I sniffle.

Papa reaches over again and squeezes my leg. "You are not *just* a kid. You are our Princess with a superpower that spreads JOY. I knew you would help the rest of the kingdom by coming here, but I was also hoping some of your spirit would rub off on the queen."

I look up. "That's not gonna happen! And even though she's given us nice rooms in the palace and lets us ride in her fancy coach, I miss playing with my friends. And I know you and Mama miss our farm."

"We do." Papa thinks for a minute and then takes a deep breath. "I think it's time for me to have a talk with the queen and let her know you have done your job here, and it's time for us to return to our village. But for now . . ."

Papa stops talking and taps loudly on the roof of the carriage. "Driver, stop the coach!" He yells.

Mama and I give each other a puzzled look.

The coach rolls to a stop, and Papa opens the door. "Everybody out!" He orders. Then he jumps out and lifts me and then Mama to the ground. "Driver, we are going to walk the rest of the way to the palace. It's too nice a day to ride."

The coachman looks a bit startled, but he smiles. "As you wish, sir. Enjoy your stroll." Then he flicks the reins, and the horses trot off.

Papa whispers something to Mama, and she smiles and nods. I turn around to walk back. I can see the palace, and I can feel the sun on my bald head.

"Wait a minute, Princess," Papa calls. "Your mother and I may not be Mia and Henry, but we can still have a little fun. We are not just going to walk back. We are going to fly!"

I look at Papa like he's gone crazy.

Mama giggles. "I am going to be a butterfly!" She stretches out her arms and flutters them.

"And I am a fierce dragon," Papa bellows. "I can fly and breathe fire at the same time." He stretches out his arms and snorts. At least, I think that is what he is trying to do. It is sort of a weird sound coming from his nose and mouth.

I can't help it. I start giggling, too.

Mama, who is still fluttering, asks me, "And what will you be, Joy?"

It only takes a moment for me to decide. "I'm a fairy!" I stretch out my wings and dance around a bit. "You can call me Faerygale!"

"What a great name!" Mama laughs as she and Papa start "flying" down the road.

"Wait for me!" I fly to catch up with them.

This is so totally crazy! I love my family. I feel lighter and happier than I have for weeks. We must look like we are out of our minds.

As we approach the palace, I glimpse the sparkle of a crown at one of the windows. The queen! She is watching us. So, let her! Let her see what Joy looks like, and I don't mean me.

We all stop at the gate, laughing and a little out of breath.

"Look," I point up to the window. My parents look up. They just manage to catch the sparkle before it vanishes from the window. But Papa points further up to the sky.

"Oh my," he whispers. "That cloud over the palace *does* look like a dragon."

We are all looking up when a guard rushes out of the palace. "Joy! You there, Joy! The queen wishes to see you immediately! I will escort you."

Whoa. The queen wishes to see me? She hasn't said two words to me since I've been here. Will she be as mean as I remember? My heart starts beating faster.

Thump, Thump. Thump, Thump!

"I'd like to have a word with the queen," Papa starts.

"Later! The queen only wishes to see Joy at this time," the guard insists.

Papa frowns. He's about to object, but I say, "It's okay, Papa. I'll be fine." I'm surprised my voice isn't shaking. I start to go with the guard but then turn back.

"Thanks for the flying lessons. I really do feel so much better. You are the best!" I give them both a quick hug.

"If you ever need a dragon, you know where to find one!" Then Papa snorts.

I giggle. The guard rolls his eyes. And I'm off to meet with the queen.

Chapter 2

The door closes behind me, and I am alone with the queen in one of her chambers. Her back is to me. The room is so dark and gloomy that I can barely see. There is a stained glass window to the right. That must be where I saw her.

Before I can speak, she whirls around, glares at me, and points to the open window. "What in the world were you and your parents doing just now?"

I take a moment to catch my breath. The queen looks even younger than I remember. And her hair! All that silver, swishy hair!

With a perfectly straight face I say, "Flying."

"What?" she chokes out.

"They were pretending to be a dragon and a butterfly, and I was pretending to be a fairy, and we were flying down the road."

"Well, you all looked perfectly ridiculous," she sputters.

"We were just having fun, something you wouldn't know about."

As soon as the words are out of my mouth, I regret them. The queen looks like she's been hit or something.

“I’m sorry,” I apologize. “My parents were just trying to cheer me up. I miss my friends, Mia and Henry, and we used to race and run all the time going home.”

“I see. Well, you are right. I don’t know about having fun. I’m a queen with important decisions to make. And if I make a mistake or feel sad, I don’t have any parents to *cheer me up*.”

I remember that Faerygale told me that the queen probably gets angry at herself because she makes mistakes, but I’m not about to bring up my guardian fairy in my dreams. She really would think I am crazy. But I do know why she is sad.

“I’m sorry. My mother told me that you lost both of your parents when you were about my age. That’s got to be really tough.”

“It was.” The queen looks at me and shakes her head. “But you can’t possibly understand that. You’ve always had your parents.”

“Well, no, actually. I didn’t always have my parents.” I then tell her that I was found.

“So, they adopted you. But don’t you ever wonder who your real parents are?” She asks.

“Not really. My *real* parents are right here in the palace. They love me, and I love them. Being adopted was like the first step of my life, and my life has been pretty great ever since.”

"Yes, and now you have a superpower which makes everyone love you. No wonder you have a lot of friends. Some people have all the luck." She looks away.

"Talk about luck! You are the queen! You can have anything you want. You could have tons of friends."

"Queens don't have friends. We have subjects." She turns her back to me.

"That's ridiculous," I mutter.

"What?" She whips around to face me.

"I know everybody can have friends, even a queen. But you just like being mean to everyone, calling people names, bossing everyone around."

"I'm the queen! It's my job to boss people around. And I don't call people names." She practically shouts this.

"You called me Baldy!"

She stops what she is about to say and stares at me a moment. Then her whole face changes. She looks kind of sad. She turns and goes to the window. I can barely hear her. It's like she is talking to herself. "I did. That was wrong. My mother would be so ashamed of me. What's wrong with me?"

I move to stand beside her. I don't know what to say. I try to think of what Mama would say. I put my hand on her arm. "My mother would say, *You are perfect just as you are,* but then she would probably ground you."

The queen cracks a smile, and then she actually laughs!

"*My* mother would have said something very similar. And then my *father* would have grounded me." She takes my hand, "But first they would have made me apologize. I'm sorry for calling you a name."

This is so weird. The queen is apologizing to me?

"Well, uh, thanks." I shake her hand because I don't know what else to do. Then I think of a way to change the subject.

"Let's start over. Hi, my name is Joy. What's yours?" I feel really silly saying it, but it's all I can think of since she is holding my hand.

She gives me a strange look, but then shakes my hand and says, "Hi Joy, my name is Star. Nice to meet you." Then we both let go at the same time.

Wow, the queen just told me her name. And she smiled at me!

Awkward silence.

I look out the window and see the sun setting through the clouds. "Hey, look at that cool sunset. I really like all the shades of orange, although I think the sunrise colors are my favorite."

The queen, I mean Star, gazes at the sky. "My favorite color is dark blue, like the night sky," she says.

"Yeah, I can tell," I say. "Dark blue really shows off your silver hair. It's very pretty. For a long time, I wished I had pretty hair, but now I'm used to not having any."

The queen shifts her gaze to me. "I don't mean to be rude, but why are you bald?"

"I have no idea. I've just been this way all my life. I used to get teased, and it bothered me a lot. But not anymore. Why is your hair silver? You're not old or anything."

"I have no idea. It's been this way since I was born. That's how I got my name. My mother said my hair reminded her of silver stars."

"My parents called me Joy because they couldn't have kids, and when they found me, I was their Joy."

"My name is unusual, just like my hair, but I sort of like it. I think our parents picked out good names," Star says. And for once, she looks at ME and not just my bald head!

"You know, as queen, I could put the people who teased you in our dungeon for a while."

"What? Are you kidding?"

"Yes," she laughs. "I mean I could, just to teach them a lesson."

I realize it could be really great having a queen for a friend. But then I tell her, "That might work for some people, but I found out that being kind turns bullies into friends."

"Really?" Star looks interested.

"Yes." Then we sit down, and I explain how Henry used to bully me but is now one of my best friends.

Star listens and for the first time I notice how pretty her face is, when she's not frowning or acting mean.

There is another moment of silence, but it's not awkward this time.

"You know," Star begins. "There's something I've been thinking about since that day in your village when you sang that song. It sounded very familiar. Where did you learn it?"

"Oh, that's *my* song. I learned it from my mother. She first heard it the day . . ."

There is a loud knock on the door of the chamber.

"Wait a moment," Star says to me. "Enter," she calls out.

The door opens, and a guard enters. "Your majesty, visitors have just arrived. Two children and two adults. They told me to tell you their names were Henry and Mia."

"What?" I jump up. "Henry and Mia, here! Yay!"

I'm so excited that I forget to say goodbye to the queen. I run past the startled guard and out the door shouting, "Henry, Mia!"

Chapter 3

I race down the stairs. I can't wait to see my best friends.

"Joy!" Mia runs to meet me and gives me a hug so big we both burst into giggles.

Henry laughs, too. "Hey, don't squeeze her to death!"

We have a zillion things to talk about. We start talking at the same time.

"How did you get here?"

"How are you?"

"How is everyone back home?"

"Have you finished singing to the farms?"

Henry shakes his head and interrupts us. "Time out! I can't understand who is asking what. I think I heard one question. Mia's parents brought us in their wagon."

"But who is looking after our farm?" I ask.

"Henry's parents! Everyone in the village offered. They all wanted to thank you for helping them. Everything is fine at home," Mia explains.

"I am sooo glad to see you guys! I was really missing you," I say.

"Mia said you were, and you needed us. She convinced her parents that they should take her to the palace. And she talked them into letting me come along." Henry looks at Mia. "I don't know how she does it, but she knows things before other people know them."

"I know! I've told her that is her superpower!" I exclaim.

Mia shrugs and says, "It's no big deal. I just knew if I had been away from you for a long time, I would be missing you and would really like a visit."

Henry nods, "That's called *empathy*."

Mia and I stare at Henry. Since when does Henry use big words?

"Aw, come on! Stop staring," he laughs. My mom told me that *empathy* is when you can put yourself in another person's shoes, so you know exactly how they feel. I thought it was a cool word, so I remembered it."

"That's impressive, Henry," I tell him.

"Yeah, I guess I have "em-pa-thy," Mia says carefully. "But it's not a superpower because anyone can have THAT. It's not like Henry's power. Henry saved us coming here."

"What? Sit down and tell me everything." We all sit on the stairs.

"I'm still not sure myself what happened," Henry starts.

"Oh please. I know exactly what happened," Mia interrupts. "We were all in the wagon, and it was getting dark. The horse started to get jittery, and just then I saw two glowing eyes leap at the horse."

"It was a wolf, a pretty big one," Henry explains. "He spooked the horse."

"Daddy was holding onto the reins trying to control the horse, and Mom was screaming. Henry threw out his arms and somehow knocked that wolf clear back into the woods, and then it ran away. It wasn't going to bother anyone else that night on the road. Now that's a superpower!" Mia finishes.

Henry blushes. "But who told me to get ready to stand up in the wagon, even before we saw the wolf?"

"Well, I had a funny feeling something bad might happen," Mia explains.

"Mia!" I jump up. "That is your superpower! You *felt* like something might happen just like you *knew* I needed you here. Just admit you have your special power!"

"Okay, okay. Just give me a cape." She laughs and stands up, thrusting her arm out in a super hero pose.

"We all start laughing, but a frosty voice from the top of the stairs stops us. "I see you feel better now that your friends are here."

We look up to see the queen standing with a palace guard.

"Yes, I do," I say smiling. "It's so great to see them again. This is Mia and Henry. I was just telling you . . ."

"Yes, well I'm sure they would like to go to their rooms. They must be tired after their journey. Guard, see to it." She turns to leave.

"But, Star, don't you want to come down and really meet them?" I ask.

The guard gasps.

The queen looks at me coldly and says very sharply, "Just because you know my name doesn't mean you can use it." She marches off.

The guard says to Mia and Henry, "I will show you to your rooms now."

Mia and Henry start up the stairs. I'm still a little shocked by Star's—I mean the queen's—sharp tone. I just stand there.

Mia comes back down and grabs my hand. "You're coming with us. We still have a LOT to talk about." Then she whispers, "I can't wait to hear all about *Star*." Then she winks at me and pulls me up the stairs.

Chapter 4

"I thought we had a lot of food in our village now," Henry says as he plops down in a huge chair. "But last night's dinner was a feast! And this morning, I have never seen so many dishes for breakfast in my life. Of course, I had to have one of each kind of muffin: blueberry, cherry, mickleberry, . . ."

"Okay stop already. I'm too full to even *hear* about food!" Mia exclaims. "I thought Star would be eating with us. But I haven't seen her since she yelled at you on the stairs yesterday."

"Keep calling her Star, and she'll do more than yell. We could all end up in the dungeon," I warn. "Besides, the *queen* usually eats alone."

"Cool," Henry says. "I've never seen a dungeon."

We both look at him and shake our heads.

"I won't call her Star to her face," Mia says. "But after what you told us last night, I think she wishes she had us as friends."

"You guys do make great friends, even if you stuff yourselves silly," I smile.

"I think she got all snippy because she saw us together and was a little jealous," Mia adds.

"Could be," I agree. I remember what Faerygale told me in my last dream. Sometimes people are unkind because they don't have enough of something like food or friends. I look directly at Henry and say, "People can definitely be mean when they don't have something other people have." We both remember when he bullied me about my baldness. Hunger made him mean.

Henry looks down at his feet. "I'm still sorry for that. But I'm glad we are friends now."

"That's it! Star needs friends! When she has friends, I know she will feel better and be kinder," Mia states. "Now, what can we do to show her that we are her friends?"

"She obviously doesn't need food. She has plenty of food." Then Henry lets out a loud burp.

BRWAAPP

"EWW," Mia and I say at the same time.

"Sorry," Henry says. "Better to let it out and bear the shame, then keep it in and bear the pain."

"That's just gross," Mia shakes her head. "Let's get serious. We've got to think of something to do for her that's nice." She walks over to my window and looks out.

"I've been so busy visiting farms that yesterday was the first time we really talked," I tell her.

"We could see that you've been singing," Henry assures me. "In every town and village on our way here, the sun was shining and crops were growing. But you know, it was sort of strange. When we got here, it seemed like dark clouds were hanging over the palace."

Suddenly Mia turns around, "I've got it! Come over here and look outside." She motions for us to look out the window.

Henry and I rush over.

"What do you see?" Mia asks.

"Dark clouds," says Henry, as he looks up.

"A dead garden," I say as I look down.

"Exactly!" Mia exclaims. She looks really excited. "Joy, I bet you have not sung here, yet, right?"

She's right. I'm starting to catch on, and I nod my head and grin.

"Then let's get going!" Mia commands.

"Where?" Henry asks completely lost.

"To the garden, silly. Joy is going to sing in that garden to make it beautiful and to knock these dark clouds out of here. Then when the queen sees her own palace beautiful and knows we did it, she will know she has friends. Let's go!"

Henry gets there first. He is a superfast runner. But Mia and I are right behind.

"Let me . . . catch . . . my breath," I gasp out, half laughing.

We walk over to a stone bench in the middle of the saddest excuse for a garden I have ever seen. There is enough room for all three of us to sit and wait for our hearts to stop racing.

Henry speaks first, "This place is really dead. Even the weeds have died."

"Yeah, it's . . . creepy looking. I can see why no one comes out here," Mia agrees. "But that's going to change right now. Start singing Joy!"

I stand up and close my eyes and start singing my song.

Shine on, Little One.
Shine your light so bright!
Shine on like the sun
in the dark of night!
The joy your light brings
Makes me want to sing!
Shine on as an angel of the light!

I finish the song and open my eyes. Instead of weeds, there is soft green grass with beds of flowers of every color. There are even vines with fat juicy grapes. This never gets old.

"Yeah, now this is what I'm talking about," Mia says twirling around.

"These grapes are awesome!" Henry says as he grabs a bunch and starts to eat them.

"Henry, how can you possibly put anything more in your stomach?" Mia asks.

"I'm a growing boy," he replies.

"Shh!" I whisper. "I hear someone coming. Quick! Hide!"

We dash behind the thickest flowering bush.

We hear a guard say, "I saw them go out into the garden, Your Majesty, and I thought you should know."

Then we see the queen enter the garden. We huddle closer and watch her slowly walk over to the bench. We all seem to hold our breaths as we wait for her reaction. Maybe she'll actually smile again. But then her shoulders start to shake. She puts her hands up to her face.

She's crying. Oh no! Why?

"Let's get out of here," Henry whispers, and we carefully inch our way back to the garden door. The sky is already getting darker. Just as we get to the door, I feel a large drop of rain on my head.

We race back to my room. All three of us go to the window and look down on the garden. The queen is still sitting on the bench, getting drenched.

"Why is she still sitting there?" Henry asks.

"Forget that, why did she start crying?" Mia wonders.

"Tears of joy?" Henry offers.

"More like tears Joy caused." I feel so bad. I would rather have the queen angry than sad.

"Okay, so something went wrong. We can still fix this." Mia starts pacing around the room. "Think, think, think," she mutters. "What can we do?"

All at once, she stops and stares at the hook on my door that has my rainbow scarf hanging on it.

She grabs the scarf. "Quick, Joy, take your scarf down to her. Give it to her to put on her head."

"What?" Henry asks confused.

"Just do it!" Mia thrusts the scarf into my hand. "Go!"

I'm not sure what good this will do, but I trust Mia. I take the scarf and run back down and out into the pouring rain.

The queen is still sitting on the bench. It's like she doesn't even care that she is soaking wet.

I walk over to her. "Uh, sorry to interrupt, but it's raining, and I thought you could use a scarf."

The queen doesn't even look at me. "You did this, didn't you?" She gestures to the garden.

I want to hide again, but I tell her the truth. "Yes, I thought it would make you happy."

"The garden hasn't looked like this in a very long time," she says softly.

Doesn't she realize it's raining? Drops are running down my forehead and dripping off my nose! "Here," I put the scarf right in front of her face. "Your hair is getting pretty wet. Put this on."

The queen finally focuses on the scarf. Her face turns pale, and her eyes open wide. Then with one hand she grabs the scarf, and with the other she grabs my arm.

"Where did you get this?" She shakes the scarf in my face and stands over me.

"It's my scarf. I didn't steal it. I've had it since I was a baby."

She's not letting go, and I'm starting to get scared. "That's the scarf I was wrapped in when my mother found me. Ouch! Let go!"

Instantly, she drops my arm. She stares at me and then stares at the scarf and then at me again.

"Oh, No! No, No!" She races out of the garden and back into the palace, clutching my scarf and leaving me standing in the rain.

Chapter 5

Why does everything always go wrong when it comes to the queen? Mia and Henry saw what happened in the garden. They were as confused as I was, and they even argued about it. Henry told Mia that her idea turned out to be terrible. Mia told him that at least she tried. All he ever did was think about his stomach. Then they both left my room, saying they wanted to be alone. Fine.

Now I'm lying on my bed, trying to figure out what went wrong. It's been raining all day. Let it rain. I don't feel like singing. I just want to leave this place and go home.

There's a soft knock on my bedroom door. I really don't want to talk to anybody, but I say, "Come in."

It's Mama and Papa. I sit up.

Mama begins, "I'm not sure what happened today, but talking about it usually makes things clearer." She comes over to sit on the bed. Papa stands at the foot.

I doubt if anything will change, but I tell them what happened in the garden and then with Mia and Henry afterwards.

"I wouldn't worry too much about Mia and Henry. Even friends have disagreements. But then they get over it," Mama says. "I'm sure they will work things out."

Papa is frowning slightly. "It's time," he states. "We are going back home, whether she likes it or not. I'm talking to the queen in the morning. Don't worry any more, Princess. I'll take care of it." He gives me a quick kiss on my bald head and goes out the door.

"Well, I guess that's that. I must say that I miss the farm, and I'll be glad to get back home," Mama says. "But for now, I would like you to eat a little something. I'm going to bring up a tray."

Home! I'm going home! That makes me feel better, but I'm still worried about what's going on with my friends. And I'm still trying to figure out what happened with the queen.

I'm lost in thought when there's another knock on my door, and it opens. I'm surprised to see Mia walk in, wearing her nightgown. Mama is right behind her. "I thought since this might be our last night in the palace that you might like to have a sleepover! I brought hot chocolate, cookies, and some mickleberries."

"All my favorites!" Mia exclaims as she crawls into the other side of the big bed.

"Just be careful not to spill anything." Mama kisses me and turns to leave.

Just as she is about to close the door, she turns and says, "I know you have a lot to talk about, just try NOT to stay up all night. Tomorrow could be a big day. Good night."

"We won't," I promise.

"Good night," Mia calls out, "and thanks for the snacks!"

Now that we are alone, we are both quiet, which is super strange. I pass her a cup of hot chocolate.

"Thanks," she says.

I take a sip of mine. She blows a bit on hers.

She looks at me. "You have a totally marshmallow mustache," she giggles and takes a sip of hers.

I lick my upper lip. "So do you!"

"Twins!" We both laugh, and I relax. It's good to be laughing with her again.

Mia begins, "I still can't figure what happened today. I thought for sure that garden would make Star happy. And I got a very strong feeling that she should have that scarf when it started to rain. But boy, was I wrong."

"I don't blame you. We tried."

We quietly munch some cookies, careful not to get too many crumbs in the bed.

"You remember what Faerygale said in my dream. She sort of said that the queen's sadness and anger caused the Darkness in the first place," I remind her.

Mia nods, "Yeah, I remember you telling me about that dream. No wonder this palace stays dark, with her living here. So, probably nothing we can do will change her, until she changes herself. Hey, have you had any more Faerygale dreams since you've been here?"

"Nope. Haven't had any dreams at all," I reply.

"So, no word about you being a real princess?"

"Nope. I mean I'm living in a castle. Papa still calls me Princess, but that's about it. I've been so busy lately that I haven't thought about it much." I sip my hot chocolate. It's yummy. "Have you talked with Henry since he left us?" I ask.

"Not really," she replies.

“Mama says that all friends fuss, so maybe you guys just need a little time.”

“Mmm,” she nods with a mouth full of mickleberries.

“Speaking of friends, tell me more about everyone at home. I’m tired of talking about the queen and this place. What’s been going on since we left?”

Mia fills me in about our village, and the hours tick by. The last thing I remember I am sinking down onto my pillow. I think Mia is talking about Faerygale again.

Chapter 6

I'm so sleepy, but Mia just asked me a question. I open my eyes to answer her, but I am no longer in the bed. I'm in a meadow. The same meadow from my past dreams with the familiar butterflies. Yay! I need a good dream and can't wait to see Faerygale again. But where is she?

"Faerygale!" I shout. "It's me, Joy. Where are you?"

I don't hear any reply, but I do hear faint music. It's my song! The butterflies are fluttering in the direction of the music, so I follow them.

I seem to walk a long time, and the field sort of changes into a garden. It really looks like the garden at the palace. It is! And there on the bench is my guardian fairy, Faerygale! She looks so pretty. If I had hair, I would want it to be the same as hers, with all the colors of the rainbow. Her wings sparkle in the sunlight, and she smiles at me and motions for me to come sit beside her.

I run towards her and give her a big hug when I sit beside her.

"My goodness! What a wonderful welcome that is. There is nothing like a good hug to make us feel better," she laughs that tinkling, musical laugh of hers.

"I am sooo glad to see you," I begin. "So much has happened since our last visit."

"I know," she looks at the butterflies around me. "Remember, my butterflies are always with you, even if you can't see them." As she says this, two Monarch butterflies land on her shoulders. "They love you as much as I do, and they let me know everything that happens to you and others."

"Then you know that I've been doing what you asked me to do. I've been singing everywhere. Most of the Darkness in the Kingdom is gone," I explain.

"But not at the palace," she says softly.

I sigh, "No, total failure there."

Faerygale places her hand on my leg, and the two butterflies flutter over to my shoulders. "Joy, I am so proud of you. You left your home when you didn't want to. You sang for strangers when you weren't sure they would like you. You tried to help the queen. All that took courage."

"We thought for sure bringing back the garden would make the queen happy, and the dark clouds over the palace would go away. But it made her cry! And then giving her my scarf just upset her more. I don't understand."

"In time all will be revealed, and you will understand. But for now, please know as much as you would like to, it is not your job to make Star happy. Only she has the power to do that," Faerygale says.

"That's sort of what Mia said." I am so confused. I look at her and shake my head. "But you said my singing would bring joy to people."

"And it did! Your singing brought back the sunshine and made the crops grow. Many people in the Kingdom are happier today for it. But you and your parents were happy even before your singing, right?"

"Yeah, pretty much. We still laughed a lot." I nod my head.

"You chose to be happy. You had terrible crops and not much money, but you chose happiness. Are you starting to see?" Faerygale looks at me with those dark, almond eyes.

"But why would anybody, especially a queen, choose to be unhappy? This just doesn't make sense." I shake my head.

"It is very hard to understand," Faerygale agrees with me. "Everyone has a right to be sad or angry at times. But Star has chosen to let sadness and anger rule her life."

"If that's her choice, what can I do? What can anyone do for someone like that?"

"Forgive her."

"What?"

"Forgive her for being sad. Forgive her for being angry. Don't let sadness and anger make YOU sad or angry."

"Okay, but I don't see how that is going to help her," I shake my head.

"Maybe one day she will be able to forgive herself and let herself be happy."

"Maybe. But I still feel bad that I upset her even more." I hang my head. Then I feel the wings of the two butterflies seem to kiss my cheeks.

"What is it that your mother is always telling you, especially when you feel down about yourself?" Faerygale takes my hands into hers.

I raise my head and think for a second. "You are perfect, just as you are? Is that what you mean? You said it to me before, too," I add.

"Yes! And are you perfect?"

Is this a trick question? "Well, no. I make mistakes. Everybody does!"

"Exactly. So, what do you think we *really* mean when we say that?" Faerygale squeezes my hands harder, and the butterflies brush my bald head with their wings. I feel safe and loved.

THAT'S IT! Love!

"It's a way of saying that you love me just the way I am!"

"YES!" Faerygale is beaming, and the two butterflies seem to dance between her and me. "Your mother and I know you make mistakes, but we also know you are sorry for them and do your best to correct them. We will always be there for you when you do that. Then she says in a quieter voice, "When do you think was the last time someone was there for Star? When do you think she heard words like *You are perfect just as you are*?"

I frown a little, remembering what Star told me the other day. "I guess it's been a long time--maybe since her parents died?" The butterflies land on Faerygale's hand.

Faerygale lifts her hand and seems to talk to them. "Parents are not the only ones who can be there for us." Then she looks directly at me. "When Star sees that you care enough to forgive her, perhaps that will remind her that she is loved."

Faerygale doesn't wait for me to say anything. She waves the butterflies into the air and pulls me off the bench into a big hug.

"I love you, Princess Joy!

I try to hug her back, but she's vanished.

"Wake up Joy, wake up!"

My eyes fly open to find Mia staring down at me. "You were having a dream! Start at the beginning and tell me EVERYTHING!"

Chapter 7

I tell Mia everything I can remember before we are interrupted.

"Joy, Mia, time to get up!" Mama quickly enters the room. "Oh good, you're awake. Mia, your mom wants to talk to you right away. Henry has been knocking on their door, bothering them since dawn. He wants to talk with you. And Joy, you get dressed quickly. The queen wants to see you immediately. She won't even talk to your father, until she talks to you." She turns and rushes back out.

Mia and I both jump out of bed. "Wow, first the dream and now this. And it's not even breakfast!" Mia exclaims.

She starts for the door. Then she hurries back to give me a quick hug. "Good luck," she whispers.

"I'll need it," I reply. "And good luck with Henry."

She laughs," I won't need luck. We will be fine." And she's out the door.

I get dressed superfast and go out to the hallway, where Mama and Papa are waiting for me. Together we walk to the queen's chambers.

Just outside her door, Papa turns to me. "All right Princess, remember, if you need a dragon, I'll be right here." And he gives a big snort.

He always knows how to make me laugh.

"I think I'll be okay, but I'm glad you'll be close by."

I walk into the same room as yesterday. The door shuts behind me. The queen is standing by the fireplace.

She turns to me. She is very pale, and I'm surprised to see my scarf in her hands.

"Please have a seat, Joy."

She said "please," and she doesn't sound angry. I think maybe everything will be all right.

I sit down. "Listen, about yesterday, . . ." I begin.

"No," she cuts me off. "Joy, I have something to tell you, and I can't be interrupted. You need to listen to me. What I have to say is very . . . important."

I stop talking.

She continues. "Yesterday we talked a little about parents. I remember mine. I loved them very much, and they loved me. Papa would tell me stories, and he taught me how to ride. Mama would sing to me right out there in that garden and play games with me. I was literally the *Star* of the palace. Papa was a great king. He was kind and brave. He died while saving others in a fire."

I nodded. That's what Mama had told me.

"I don't know if you know this, but before Papa died, Mama found out she was going to have a baby. We were all so excited. I had always wanted a baby brother. I just knew it was going to be a boy. But after Papa died, Mama changed. A sort of darkness came over her. She didn't want to go out into the garden, or sing, or play games with me. I tried to make her happy, but I couldn't. She just got sadder and sadder."

I remember Mama telling me that people said that Star's mother had died of a broken heart, and there were rumors of a baby.

The queen took a deep breath here. "What I'm about to tell you has been a secret for years."

There goes my heart again. *Thump, Thump. Thump, Thump!*

"The Kingdom thinks that Mama didn't have a healthy baby. But she did! I will never forget how beautiful that baby was and how happy Mama was. We both loved the baby right away. I thought the bad times were over. But they weren't.

"Mama had not even named the baby when she got really sad and scared again. She ordered that the baby and I be taken away in a coach, some place far from the palace. I cried and told her I didn't want to go, but Mama told me that I had to protect the baby from the Darkness. I had no idea what she meant, but I promised I would.

"Mama could barely stand. She was too sick to come with us. She sent us with the nursemaid. She wrapped the baby up and kissed both of us. I remember her last words to me were, *Shine on Star, I love you both so much.*

"My next memories are a blur. I remember the coach racing away from the palace. I don't know how long we were riding or how far away we were. The nurse had let me hold the baby. Suddenly the world was turned upside down. The coach was on its side, and my head really hurt. Still clutching the baby, I crawled out of the coach. The nurse and the driver were not moving. I had to get help.

"I did my best to carry the baby with me. I tried. I really tried, but my head hurt so badly. I thought I might drop the baby, so I found a nice place to put her down. I kissed her and told her I would be back as soon as I got help. Then I headed down the road."

Her, the baby was a girl! Thump, Thump. Thump, Thump!

"My next memory is waking up in my bed in the palace weeks later. I was told I had been in a terrible accident where everyone had perished. I was lucky I had survived. And what was worse, Mama had died and I was now queen."

Now the queen is talking superfast. "At first, I told everyone they were wrong. My mother could not have died. I had a sister. We had to find her. But they just shook their heads and said I was confused. I had a pretty bad head injury and could not remember things correctly. It got to the point I didn't know what was real, except that I was queen and had a lot to learn."

The queen finally takes a breath and turns to face me. She is crying.

"But in my dreams, I saw my baby sister. I saw her in that field, wrapped in my mother's scarf. This scarf."

She holds out the scarf, and I stand up and take it. My rainbow scarf. I look into her eyes. I can't believe what I am hearing.

I can't breathe. *Thump, Thump. Thump, Thump!*

Then she hugs me so tight, my arms are pinned at my side. "I knew I had a sister. I knew it. I should not have believed everyone. They should have believed me."

I don't hug her back right away. I'm in shock. She's my SISTER?

The queen, Star, pulls back. She sees the look on my face. "I am so sorry! It's all my fault. I should have tried harder to find you. Can you ever forgive me?"

I am silent.

"Please say something," Star sobs.

I look at her and for a moment I think I see Faerygale on the mantle behind her. But then I blink, and Faerygale is gone.

"I forgive you."

Star stares at me through her tears.

"But I need to go now." And I run out the door.

Chapter 8

"Oh my goodness," Mama says softly as she strokes my head.

"This is unbelievable," Papa says. "I'm not sure I can believe it."

We are all quiet for a moment as I stop sniffling. I told them everything. They are as stunned as I am.

"What did you say to her?" Mama asks.

"I didn't know what to say. But then *I forgive you* just came out of my mouth."

"You forgive her?" Papa stands up.

Mama smiles at me. "Of course, you do. We all must. She was just a child. After all, if Joy had not been put in that field, I would never have found her."

"But she's a princess! This is her palace as much as it is the queen's," Papa points out. "Everything will change now."

"I may be a princess, but I'm still Joy. You are still my parents. Everything doesn't need to change. Right?" My voice sounds shaky.

"Oh Joy, you are our child now and will always be!" Mama says, and they both give me a big hug.

Whoa! It sinks in. I am a REAL PRINCESS. Faerygale was right.

There's a soft knock on the door.

Papa opens it, and there is Star.

"May I come in?" she asks. She is carrying a large box.

Papa doesn't say anything, but Mama says, "Of course, come right in."

Star comes in and puts the box on the table. "By now Joy has told you everything."

Mama and Papa nod.

"I am so very sorry. I don't know what you think of me, but you can never blame me as much as I blame myself." She hangs her head.

Mama goes to her. "You were just a child. You tried your very best in a very scary situation, just like I did my best trying to find Joy's parents. Sometimes things don't work out, but we don't have to blame ourselves for the rest of our lives. We all forgive you. Now you must forgive yourself."

I stare at my mother. That's exactly what Faerygale and I had talked about.

Star lifts her head, and there are tears in her eyes. "How can you forgive me?"

Mama smiles, "In a way, you gave us Joy. And our lives have been blessed ever since."

"And we don't plan to give her up, even if she is your sister and the princess," Papa speaks up.

"I understand how you feel. And you don't have to give her up. There's plenty of room in the palace. You can all live here now," Star says hopefully.

Mama and Papa look at each other. Then they look at me.

I don't know what to say. Live in the palace? WOW! But I would miss our farm and be so far away from Mia and Henry.

Papa starts, "This is a very big decision. We will have to talk it over as a family."

"Of course," Star says. "Take all the time you want. But I have a surprise for Joy." She goes to the big box and brings it to me. "I had the dressmakers work all night. This is for you!"

I look at Mama and Papa, and they nod their heads. I tear into the box.

I can't believe it. It's THE dress—from my dreams with Faerygale.

"How? How did you know about this dress?" I ask Star.

"I'm not sure about the exact design. I think I dreamed it. But I knew it should be in your favorite colors."

What? *She dreamed it?*

"It's perfect!" I exclaim.

"And here is your princess crown!" Star shuffles through the tissue and brings out the tiara, ALSO from my dream! "The jewelers worked all night, too." Star places it on my head.

Mama and Papa have such silly, surprised looks. Kind of like the first time they watched me sing to our fields.

I hold the dress up in front of me and turn to the mirror to look. Star leans up next to me to look, too. I gasp! I have never noticed how much we look alike.

We ARE sisters!

Suddenly, the door flings open. "Hey Joy!" Mia barges in. "Just wait 'til I tell you. . ." She stops. She takes one look at Star and me and says, "Holy Moly!"

We all laugh. Thank goodness. I needed a good laugh about now.

"Well, I know I've given you a lot to think about. Please let me know what you decide as soon as possible." Star starts to leave, then turns and gives me a big hug, squishing my dress up against me. Then she walks out, actually smiling at Mia.

"I knew it!" Mia exclaims.

"Knew what?" Papa asks.

"Joy is a real princess!" declares Mia.

"How in the world could you possibly know that?" Mama asks, puzzled.

"Well, someone once told me that my superpower is knowing things without being told." Mia looks at me and laughs.

"Hmmm," says Papa, "so what am I thinking now?"

"You are thinking that I need to come back later because you have a lot to talk about right now," Mia says confidently. "Henry and I will catch you later, Joy," she says with a wink and a grin from ear to ear. They must have made up.

"That's exactly right!" Papa says amazed. "I guess everyone around here has a superpower."

"Yep, everyone does!" I laugh. "Bye Mia," I shout after her.

Mama, Papa, and I discuss everything for a very long time. Then we come up with a plan. This time Papa summons the queen.

When she enters our room, I can tell she is very nervous.

"Your Majesty," Papa begins.

"Oh, please call me Star," she says quickly.

Papa raises his eyebrows. "Star, we have come to a decision. Even though your offer is very generous, we have a life back in our village, and we are going to return there. All of us."

Star's shoulders slump. "But . . ." she begins.

"But, you and Joy are sisters. And Joy will visit you as often as you like," he adds.

My words come out in one big rush. "For now, I can stay a few weeks longer so we can get to know each other. And I'd like my friends to stay, too. I think you will like them. Then once school starts, I can visit whenever we have breaks. If that is okay with you?"

Before Star can speak, Mama adds, "You are now part of our family. In a way, it will be good for the Kingdom to have you at one end as queen and Joy at the other as princess. Everyone can get to know the royal family."

Star is quiet. "It's not what I wanted," she says slowly.

Uh oh. I hope she's not about to get angry.

"But it's better than what I hoped for."

Whew!

She walks over to me. "I never gave up hoping I would find my sister. Sometimes I would even dream about what you would be like. But I never imagined you would be this special."

Boy, I can't wait to talk to her about our dreams!

"Actually, I think YOU are pretty special. In fact, I think you are perfect, just as you are! After all, you ARE my sister." I give her a big hug and wink at Mama.

Mama laughs. "Well, well, well, you DO remember things I tell you."

I break away from Star. "Of course, I do! The first thing you taught me was my song." I'm so happy, I start singing it.

Shine on, Little One
Shine your light so bright!

And out of nowhere, Star starts to sing with me. She knows the whole song! Mama gets teary eyed, and Papa puts his arm around her. As the last note fades, all eyes are on Star.

"That was awesome! You know my song!" I clap my hands.

Star smiles at me and says, "Actually, that was *my* song. My mother used to sing it to me. I told you it was familiar. I guess I just sort of blocked it out after I lost you."

"That's amazing!" Mama exclaims. "I heard that song when I found Joy. She was *my* bright little one. And your mother sang it to you because *you* were her shining Star." Mama shakes her head, trying to understand it.

One of these days, I'll definitely have to tell her about my dreams.

"Star, I think you should sing *our* song with me from now on. Maybe it's YOUR superpower, too!" I declare.

"I don't know about that, but I'd love to sing it with my sister anytime."

Star turns to Mama. "You remind me of my mother. I've thought a lot about what you said about forgiving myself, and I'm going to try. But first I'm going to let the Kingdom know that we have a new princess. Tomorrow Joy will officially be crowned!"

"But what will you tell everyone?" Papa asks.

"The truth. Eventually. But for now, I will tell them that she is their princess because she brought sunshine back to the Kingdom. No one will question that. They love her already." She puts her arm around me. Mama and Papa have never looked happier.

"But I didn't do it alone," I tell her. "Now that you are no longer angry and sad, just look outside."

I grab my sister's hand and race over to the window. "Look!" I exclaim. "No more clouds, and the sun is absolutely brilliant!"

"See," I say as I hug her. "We did it. Together! WE DEFEATED THE DARKNESS!"

The End

Tricia O'Neill Politte is a retired high school English and Theatre teacher (formerly Ms. V). She has always loved teaching and kids. Her first book, **The Magic Heart**, encourages kids of all ages to find the magic within them to overcome disappointment and heartache. She enjoys acting, decorating for every holiday, and celebrating good times with family and friends. She is really happy to have authored **The Bald Princess** series with her friend, Rachel, the real Princess Joy.

Rachel Rose Gray has a diverse background in performing that includes everything from opera to television, but her greatest joy is singing for children. In 2014 she founded a non-profit organization and shaved her head to become Princess Joy, The Bald Princess, to bring joy to children in hospitals. She lives in Northern Virginia with her family and their amazing rescue dog, Tinkerbell. To learn more, please visit www.baldprincessjoy.org.

CPSIA information can be obtained
at www.ICGtesting.com
Printed in the USA
LVHW070341061021
699649LV00005B/313

9 781637 650042